Pet Charms
The Muddy Puppy

by Amy Edgar
illustrated by Jomike Tejido

SCHOLASTIC INC.

To Haya Sophia - J.T.

Library of Congress Cataloging-in-Publication Data

Names: Edgar, Amy, author. | Tejido, Jomike, illustrator. • Title: The muddy puppy / by Amy Edgar ;
illustrated by Jomike Tejido. • Description: First edition. | New York, NY : Scholastic Inc., 2017. |
Series: Scholastic reader. Level 2 | Series: Pet charms ; 1 | Summary: When Molly helps a puppy that
is caught in a storm, he thanks her with a magical charm bracelet that lets her understand what animals
say, including that he needs help. Includes a charm bracelet. • Identifiers: LCCN 2016028729 | ISBN
9781338045895 (paperback) • Subjects: | CYAC: Dogs—Fiction. | Animals—Infancy—Fiction. |
Human-animal communication—Fiction. | Magic—Fiction. | Bracelets—Fiction. | BISAC: JUVENILE
FICTION / Readers / Beginner. | JUVENILE FICTION / Fantasy & Magic. | JUVENILE
FICTION / Animals / Dogs. • Classification: LCC PZ7.E225 Mud 2017 | DDC [E]—dc23 LC
record available at https://lccn.loc.gov/2016028729

10 9 8 7 6 5 4 3 2 1   17 18 19 20 21

Printed in China
First edition, January 2017
Book design by Steve Ponzo

Molly looked out the window.
"Boom!" went the thunder.
It was windy and about to storm.

Then it started to rain!
Molly heard barking.
She saw a small white dog in her yard.

She opened the door to let him in.
But the dog did not see her.
He was busy digging.

"Over here!" Molly yelled.

But the dog kept digging in the mud.

Molly saw something shiny in the hole.

The dog picked it up.

Molly dashed outside.

She scooped up the dog and raced back.

"Gosh!" said Molly.
"You are one muddy puppy."
The dog wiggled all over.

Molly giggled as she cleaned him off.
Then he held up a bracelet.
"What is this?" Molly asked.

Molly picked up the shiny bracelet.

She tried it on.

It was a perfect fit.

The bracelet glowed for just a second.
Like magic, the dog's bark turned into words!
"I dug that bracelet up just for you," he said.

"You can talk!" Molly cried.

"Of course," the dog said.

"And when you wear the bracelet,
you can understand me."

Molly's cat, Stella, walked by.
"Cool bracelet," Stella meowed.
Molly could understand cats, too!
Her eyes widened in surprise.

Molly rushed over to the fishbowl.
She watched her fish play tag.
"You can't catch me!" she heard one goldfish say.

"Tag! You're it!" bubbled another.

"Wow!" Molly said.

"This really <u>is</u> a magic bracelet."

"The storm is over," the dog barked.

He wagged his tail.

Molly scratched between his ears.

"I will walk you home," Molly said.

"I don't have a home," said the dog.

"Oh no," said Molly.

"Let's go see my Aunt Vera.

She will know what to do."

The two friends walked outside.

"My name is Molly," she said.

"What is your name?"

"I don't have one," said the dog.

"Then we will choose a good one," Molly said.

"How about 'Mr. Wiggles'?"

"I love it!" said Mr. Wiggles.

He wiggled all over.

Molly rang the bell.

"Hello, Molly," said Aunt Vera.

"Who is your new friend?"

"Meet Mr. Wiggles," said Molly.

"Nice to meet you," said Aunt Vera.

"Welcome to Paws Palace."

Paws Palace
A home for rescued animals

Paws Palace was always noisy.
But today, the noises were different.
Molly could <u>understand</u> everything!

A canary told a joke to a cockatoo.

A hamster sang a song.

Three kittens meowed, "Look at the new puppy."

Molly sat down with Aunt Vera.
Mr. Wiggles climbed up on Molly's lap.
"Mr. Wiggles needs a home," said Molly.

"I have an idea," said Aunt Vera.
"Your friend could live here."
Mr. Wiggles barked loudly.

"That means 'Yes, please!'" Molly said.
She liked how the bracelet let her understand him.
Mr. Wiggles was so happy he wiggled all over.

Molly smiled.

She loved to visit Paws Palace.

Now she would love visiting even more.

It was time to go.

Molly started to take off the magic bracelet.

But Mr. Wiggles barked "Wait!"

"That is your bracelet now," he said.
"Thank you!" Molly said.
She gave him a big hug.

Molly waved good-bye.

Then she saw the bracelet sparkle brightly.

Molly blinked and saw something new . . .

A charm hung from the bracelet!
It was shaped like a dog.
It looked just like Mr. Wiggles.

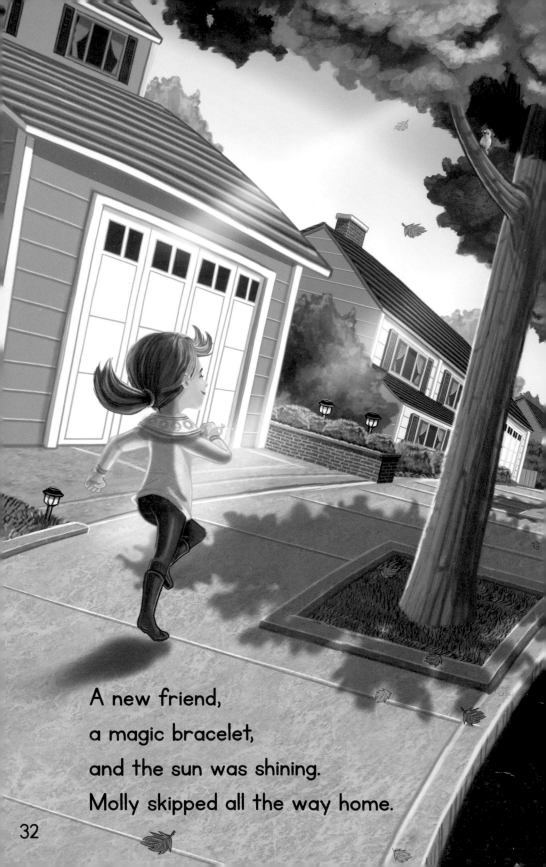

A new friend,
a magic bracelet,
and the sun was shining.
Molly skipped all the way home.